What does your sr  j ?

SMALL VOICE Says

by Mackenzie and Mike Morrison, Ph.D.
Illustrated by Nina Summer

Meet Angela.

She is seven years old.

She lives in a small apartment in a big city.

More than anything, she loves to be outside.

Her favorite place is the beach.
It's only two blocks away!

Playgrounds are just too small for Angela's big spirit. Her heart beats faster and faster as she dances at the water's edge.

When Angela's energy and the
sunlight both start to fade, it is
time to join her parents on the blanket.

Angela can sense how the beach helps
her parents to relax.
It's her favorite family time.
It's also a good time to talk.

One day, Angela asked:

Mom, can I tell you something?

Mom, I broke your favorite cup yesterday. I threw it in the trash so you wouldn't notice. I'm so, SO SORRY!

Mom pulled her close.
"Oh Angela. I am so glad you told me. Don't worry, I can get another cup. I could tell there was something that was bothering you. But your small voice wouldn't let it go."

It's how we talk to ourselves when something's up.

Something's up when we don't feel right about things.

Mom shared her own story.

"I will never forget the time I took a small piece of candy from the store. I put it in my pocket when my mom wasn't looking.

I felt bad the whole way home.

When we feel that way, it means our small voice is trying to tell us something."

Overtime, Angela's small voice helped her do new things, like learning to share with Lucy. Lucy was two years younger than Angela. She lived in the apartment across the hall.

They loved to play together.

One time, Lucy insisted on playing with Angela's new keyboard. However, Angela wasn't quite ready to share it.

She finally gave in but it only made her feel worse.

She went to her mom and asked if she could send Lucy home.
Mom asked: "What's up? Lucy's mom won't be home for an hour."

"Do your best, sweetie. Just one more hour." Mom answered.

When Angela returned to Lucy, the keyboard had been put back in its case.

Angela started to get that bad feeling.
Her small voice said, "Lucy is like your little
sister and now her feelings are hurt."

"I don't want you to go home. I will teach you your first song!" Said Angela.

One day Angela returned from school and Mom could sense that something was up.
"How was school today, Angela?"

Mom could tell that Angela wasn't quite ready to talk. But a little later it came out.

My small voice wanted me to go and say hi to him.

But what if he doesn't
want to talk?

What if I make him
feel worse?

My small voice didn't give up.

It kept saying . . .
Go talk to him!

But I didn't.

The new boy was in
the same spot, sitting
alone on the bench.
Angela started toward
him, with each step her
heart was beating faster.

As she got closer, the new boy looked up. . . . And smiled.
Angela smiled back.

A new friendship was about to begin.

COPYRIGHT

Gus & Jack Press
256 S Norton Ave
Los Angeles, CA 90004

First Printed January 2019
Library of Congress Cataloging-in-Publication Data
Morrison, Ph.D, Mike; Morrison, Mackenzie
Small Voice Says / by Mike Morrison, P.h.D and Mackenzie Morrison ; illustrated by Nina Summer.
p. cm.
Summary: Angela discovers an unlikely friend, her small voice.
ISBN 978-0-6920433-7-0 (hardcover)
The artwork was created with color pencils, ink, gouache and digital paints.

Mike Morrison, Ph.D.

Mike's passion centers on developing leaders at all ages, from the four-year-old entering pre-school to the corporate CEO leading a global enterprise. In today's world, we all need to lead in some way and Mike has helped to illuminate that path through three books, including The Other Side of the Card.

Mackenzie Morrison

Mackenzie is a writer and artist working in the music industry in Los Angeles, CA.

Nina Summer

Nina is a Swiss artist living in Brookyln, New York. She likes swing dancing, Tostitos and pro-wrestling. She doesn't have a favorite color, except maybe a soft yellow. You can find more of her work at www.nina-summer.com

CPSIA information can be obtained
at www.ICGtesting.com
Printed in the USA
LVHW071736210119
604674LV00018B/44/P

9 780692 043370